BARN CAT

BARN CAT

by Belle Coates

Illustrated by

ROBERT HENNEBERGER

New York

CHARLES SCRIBNER'S SONS

To my Father

BARN CAT

CHAPTER I

Fuzz and Bud lived on a farm in South Dakota. From their kitchen window they could see oceans of empty brown grass in summer. And oceans of empty snow in winter. They could see two far away farm houses, one giant cottonwood tree, and now and then a coyote. He was empty, too. Coyotes are always empty.

But the plains never seemed empty to Fuzz and Bud. They were full of surprises and wonder—such as the barn cat.

Uncle Pete was first to see the barn cat. Uncle Pete came into the kitchen with the pail of milk that winter morning just as Fuzz and Bud were sitting down to breakfast.

"There's a tramp cat out in our cow barn," he said.

"Good!" said Bud, buttering his pile of pancakes. "Let's keep him!"

"We have enough cats around here now," said Dad.

"This cat sleeps on the backs of the cows," Uncle Pete went on, washing up.

"Smart cat to pick such a warm bed," said Bud.

"What's his name, Uncle Pete?" asked Fuzz.

4

"I left that for you to find out," teased Uncle Pete. He knew that names were very important to Fuzz and Bud. Even names of tramps from the plains were important.

With Fuzz and Bud names had to *mean* something. For instance, he was called Bud because a bud is a small beginning that's growing up into something big and strong, like a cottonwood tree. And she was called Fuzz because her hair looked like cotton-wood fuzz, sun-bleached and fluffy and clean-smelling.

Fuzz and Bud finished their prunes and oatmeal and bacon and pancakes and milk. Then they hurried out to the cow barn with Uncle Pete to see the tramp cat.

CHAPTER II

They had a heifer named Fawn because she was sleek and nimble-footed and
looked just like a deer. Fawn was lying
down in her corner of the cow barn. And
there was this cat curled up on her back.

"He doesn't look like a tramp," Bud told
Uncle Pete.

Tramps are ragged and dirty. This cat's black fur coat was rich and shining. He wore a snow-white bib beneath his chin, and his feet were white and washed. His eyes were not green like other cats, but orange-colored and mysterious. His ears were short, like finger nails cut too close. And he had only two-thirds of a tail.

"Looks like he got the tips of his ears and tail frozen off some cold winter," said Uncle Pete.

"So now he's wise," said Bud. "He sleeps safe and warm on the backs of cows."

"And he picks the *best* cow for a bed, too," Fuzz pointed out. "Fawn has the softest back."

Uncle Pete snorted. "Wait till that wild heifer jumps the fence and runs off next time the notion hits her. That cat will find he's picked a bed with a bad habit."

In spite of her wild, nimble tricks and her bad habit, Fawn was their favorite cow. She could be loving and gentle, too. Bud stood up for her.

"Wait till Fawn gets a calf," he said. "Then she'll quiet down like other cows."

9

Just then the cat saw them in the barn doorway. He began to purr loudly. He worked his front claws in and out of Fawn's hide.

"He's practicing his piano lesson now," said Uncle Pete. "And humming the notes for you."

Fawn didn't care for the piano lesson. As the cat's claws went in and out it must have felt like eight pins being stuck in and out, four by four. Fawn switched her long tail smartly at the barn cat. He jumped off with a cheerful mew and trotted up to Fuzz and Bud. He rubbed against their legs and mewed and showed off, sharpening his claws on the cedar door post.

"He acts as if our cow barn is *his* place now," said Bud.

"He acts as if we're just visitors that he is entertaining," Fuzz giggled.

The cat jumped on Fawn's back again and began washing his bib. He forgot all about Fuzz and Bud.

"Here, Kitty," Fuzz coaxed.

"Kitty's a girl's name," said Uncle Pete. "Try Tom."

"Here, Tom," called Bud. But the barn cat wouldn't come.

They called every name they could think of.

"Here, Blackie."

"Here, Sox."

"Here, Stubby."

"Here, Croppy."

The barn cat went on with his washing and didn't look up. So they knew they hadn't called him the right name.

Fuzz and Bud couldn't bear not knowing the barn cat's name. Every animal on their farm must have a name. A name that fitted. Even their chickens had names that fitted. There was Peg, the hen with the wooden leg that Uncle Pete whittled for her. And Two-step, the blond chick who danced when she walked. There was Fearful, the big worried rooster, who spent his day running and hiding from the bossy bantam, Kingpin.

CHAPTER III

One morning during the holidays a wheat rancher from across the ridge stopped by the barn in his sled. He saw the barn cat asleep on Fawn's back.

"There's the Snyder cat!" he said. "They must have left him when they moved away."

"What did they call him?" Bud and Fuzz asked together.

The wheat rancher didn't know the cat's name.

"Why not call him Snyder?" Bud suggested brightly.

Fuzz shook her fluffy head no. Folks who would go off and leave a cat to shift for himself on the wintery plains didn't deserve to have him named after them. "Anyway, Snyder doesn't fit him," she said.

They had another problem about the barn cat besides wondering about his name. That was: Would their dad let them keep him? Dad had said they had enough cats around here now. He meant that the gray cat, Smokey, who slept in Dad's easy chair, was enough.

"That barn cat knows his place," said Dad one evening, tipping Smokey out of his easy chair before sitting down with his

farm journal. "A cat's place is out in the barn and not slipping into the house every time he gets a chance, to sleep in my chair."

By that they knew Dad meant to let the barn cat stay. So *that* problem was solved.

The barn cat and Smokey got along fine. So did the barn cat and Happy, the fun-loving cattle dog.

The barn cat got along with everything, especially with the cows, although Fawn was the only cow he liked for a bed. If she got tired of his piano playing and switched him off he never slept on Snoop or Guernsey or Rose Red. He liked them, all right. He walked among them, mewing sociably, rubbing against their legs, but he always came back to Fawn to sleep.

"Why not name him Choosey?" suggested Uncle Pete. "Or The-Cat-That-Adopted-a-Cow?"

Uncle Pete was always joking. He called the cow barn "Cat's Lodge."

Sometimes Fawn and the barn cat played together in the corral. Fawn would bunt him playfully, and he would pretend to scratch her nose. Then she would kick up

her nimble heels, lower her pretty head and rush at him. He would frisk up a corral post and sit there, pretending to be angry, with his black fur on end, and his short tail lashing back and forth.

One night in December Fawn grew restless and ran away. In the morning they found her tracks, light and tiny as a deer's, on the crusted snowdrift along the hayyard fence. They saw the place where she leaped the fence. Uncle Pete searched for her all that day, but he couldn't find her. At sun-

set Fawn came back. The barn cat was with her.

"The barn cat found her and brought her back to us!" cried Fuzz.

"A cat doesn't do things like that," said Uncle Pete. "A real smart cattle dog might bring a lost cow home, but not a cat. A cat doesn't know that much. The barn cat's just been out rabbit hunting and happened to get back when Fawn did."

Uncle Pete was tired and cold and cross from hunting Fawn. Fuzz and Bud didn't argue with him. But they knew what they knew. And they loved the barn cat more than ever.

CHAPTER IV

When Spring came Dad said it was about time that Fuzz and Bud learned to milk. Uncle Pete made them each a milking stool. Then he took them to the cow barn and showed them how the cow must stand with her right hind leg back so that they could sit properly before her bag. He taught them how to put their foreheads against the cow's warm flank, and how to squeeze and pull the warm milk from her bag into their pails. How to strip her by sliding thumb and fingers down without squeezing. Stripping got the last richest drop of milk.

While Fuzz and Bud were milking they
discovered that the barn cat stayed in the

cow barn for another reason besides a warm
bed. He stayed there for a warm meal, too!

While they milked Rose Red or Snoop they noticed how the barn cat would walk around the milking stool, mewing sociably. He would rub against the cow's hind legs and coax. Once, just for fun, Bud squirted a stream of milk at him. To his surprise the barn cat sat up and opened his mouth and drank it!

After that Bud and Fuzz always milked into his mouth until he got a meal. Sometimes they teased him a little by squirting the milk so hard that it spattered on his face and bib. He hated that. He would shake his head and run to the doorway and lick himself dry.

The barn cat taught Smokey to drink milk that way. Smokey's gray coat grew rich and shining, too. Milk did it.

CHAPTER V

That year they had a bad storm in
May. It began with rain. Then it changed
to snow. Uncle Pete didn't turn the cows
out to pasture that morning. They had shed
their winter coats by May. They would
suffer with cold. By night a blizzard was
sweeping over the Dakota plains. Uncle
Pete milked alone that night. He said it
was too stormy for Fuzz and Bud to go
out. "Can't see your hand in front of your
face," he said.

30

While the wind roared and shook the house, Fuzz and Bud sat at the kitchen table with their crayons and color books.

When it was time to go to bed they still had one more picture to color. A picture of a cat. They planned to make it black, with orange-colored eyes and a white bib. Someday, when they found the right name for the barn cat, they would write his name beneath the picture.

"Seems like we'll *never* find his name," said Fuzz.

Mother said they might finish coloring the picture before they came to bed. She told them to turn out the light when they were through. Then she and Dad and Uncle Pete went upstairs and Fuzz and Bud were alone.

All of a sudden they heard a cat crying outside in the storm. It wasn't Smokey. Smokey was curled up in Dad's easy chair.

"It's the barn cat!" Fuzz said.

"Can't be," said Bud. "He's asleep in the cow barn. He never comes near the house. He hates houses."

Fuzz turned her fluffy head, listening. "It's the barn cat at the back door," she said. "I know his voice."

They went to the door and opened it. Snow swirled up into their faces and made them gasp. The blizzard roared and rattled like a freight train rushing by.

CHAPTER VI

In the strip of lamplight that shone out of the open door they could see the barn cat crouched in the drifted path. His black coat was filled with snow and he held his head to one side to protect his poor frozen-off ears. His orange-colored eyes looked like balls of fire in the night. He was crying loudly. He had shed his winter coat early.

They couldn't call him. They didn't know his name. They could only look at him and hold their door and their hearts wide open.

He just crouched in the snow, and looked back at them, nameless and crying.

Bud shivered and closed the door. "He must be hurt. Maybe he can't walk."

"Poor thing!" said Fuzz. "We can't leave him out there all night. We've got to bring him in, Bud."

Bud said soberly, "People get lost in blizzards. Right in their own dooryards."

Fuzz nodded. She knew about that. Then she said, "He's only a step or two down the path. And we could carry the lantern. It would take us just a minute."

Even for a step or two down the path Fuzz and Bud put on their warm coats and

caps and mittens and leggings and ga-
loshes. They lighted the lantern. Then they
stepped out in the blizzard to bring the
barn cat in.

The wind pulled the breath right out of
their throats and almost pushed them down.
The world was full of black, cold and whirl-
ing, stinging snow.

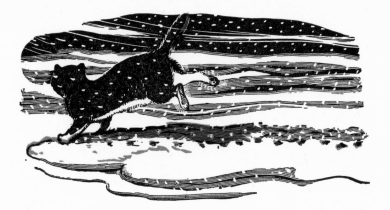

Bud held the lantern high in order to see the barn cat. The cat seemed to have moved a little farther along the path. Finally, as Fuzz stooped to pick him up, the barn cat leaped out of the drift and ran in the direction of the barn.

"He isn't hurt," Fuzz gasped, stumbling after the cat. "But the lantern scares him."

Bud caught her hand and followed with the lantern. He knew how easy it was to get lost in a blizzard, but he wasn't afraid. There was a tight woven wire fence around

the house. Only it was so terribly cold.
Already his nose was numb.

All at once they were at the cow barn,
with the barn cat leaping ahead of them
over the drifts.

"The barn door is open!" gasped Fuzz,
stopping short.

CHAPTER VII

Uncle Pete always closed the barn door at night.

Bud lifted the lantern to see. The storm had torn the barn door from its post. Snow was blowing into the cow barn, making high drifts on the floor. The milk cows stood shivering in their stanchions, their backs caked with snow.

Fawn hovered in her corner, her back turned to the wind. Now she looked like a snow-white cow.

The barn cat climbed a post beside Fawn and looked down upon her poor snow-covered back. He was still mewing loudly. Fuzz and Bud understood him now. He was telling them he couldn't sleep on an icy bed like that, and would they please do something about it.

Fawn turned her head and lowed softly. Fuzz and Bud saw something move in the drift beside her. Something small and wobbly and glistening with snow.

"It's a calf!" cried Bud. "Fawn has a new calf!"

Wonderingly, Fuzz put her mittened hand on the little calf's trembling, frosty back. "He's cold, Bud! He'll freeze to death in this open barn!"

"We've got to get Dad and Uncle Pete," said Bud.

They left the barn cat with Fawn and her calf, and started back to the house through the blizzard.

Just outside the corral gate Bud fell in a snowdrift and dropped the lantern. The light went out. They took hold of hands and stumbled across the yard through the swirling darkness.

"Here's the house!" Bud gasped at last, touching a wall. But this wall was made of logs. The house was not logs. It was made of boards. This was the chicken house. They remembered that it was only a few steps from the log chicken house to the cave, which was an outside cellar where milk and vegetables were kept. It was only a few steps from the cave to the kitchen door. It should be easy.

But they missed the cave in the storm. They bumped into the fence. Fuzz scratched her cheek on a sharp wire. She tried not to cry.

Now their feet were so stiff with cold they could hardly walk. They stumped along the fence like Peg, the wooden-legged hen. They held to each other and they held to the fence. They didn't know which way to walk, to right or to left. They were lost in their own fenced-in dooryard.

A lost feeling is a terrible feeling.

A nearly frozen feeling is a terrible feeling.

Then Bud remembered that winter wind in Dakota always came from the northwest. It should be at their backs if they were going toward the house. They turned with the wind to their backs. In another moment they reached the snow fence that stood between the yard fence and the corner of the house. It was simple to follow the snow fence to the back door.

In another moment they stumbled into the kitchen where it was light and safe and warm.

CHAPTER VIII

Fuzz and Bud hurried upstairs.

"Dad! Wake up! Fawn has a calf!"

Bud banged on Uncle Pete's door as he passed it. "Uncle Pete! Get up!"

"Where have you two been?" demanded their father from the bedroom doorway. He stared at their snowy clothes.

"At the barn," said Fuzz. "The barn door is broken off. Fawn's calf will freeze!"

Mother's face was pale. "You shouldn't have gone out in this storm!"

"I know, Mother." Fuzz ran to Mother's arms.

Bud tried to explain while Dad pulled on his boots.

"We didn't *mean* to go as far as the barn. We meant to get the barn cat and bring him out of the cold. But he led us on and before we knew it we were there. It's such a pretty calf, Dad," he said proudly.

In no time Dad and Uncle Pete set off to the barn carrying warm mash and blankets for Fawn and her calf, and tools to mend the barn door. As they left they stretched a rope from the house to the barn to hold to on their way back.

Fuzz and Bud didn't finish coloring the picture of the cat that night. They didn't wonder about his name. With Mother's help they got their icy clothes off. Then they filled hot water bottles and climbed into bed.

They knew that Dad and Uncle Pete
would soon have the barn door mended
and the storm shut out. Soon Fawn's calf
would be safe and blanketed and asleep in
warm straw, with Fawn lying contentedly
beside it, her restlessness gone now that she
had a baby. And the barn cat again would
be in his place on her warm soft back,
sleepily playing his piano tune.

Fuzz breathed a happy little sigh into her pillow. The barn cat had saved Fawn's calf. No matter what Uncle Pete said, a cat knew a lot of things. A cat like—oh, she *did* wish they knew a name for the barn cat. A wise and friendly name. A homey, barney name.

All of a sudden Fuzz had the happiest feeling she ever had in all her life. She would have gone through the blizzard all over again just to get that happy feeling.

"Bud!" she whispered excitedly. "Are you awake?"

"M-huh," mumbled Bud drowsily.

She reached out and shook him. "Listen, Bud. I know the barn cat's name! I just thought of it!"

Bud sat up, wide awake. "What is it?"

"It's Barney! Barney, for *barn* cat. It just fits him. It *can't* be anything else!"

"Naturally," said Bud. "Funny we didn't think of that before."

But then they'd never gone through a blizzard before.

Anyway, the wondering was over. The next minute Fuzz and Bud were fast asleep.